The Old Woman and the Rice Thief

adapted from a Bengali folktale

by Betsy Bang
illustrated by Molly Garrett Bang

Greenwillow Books

A Division of William Morrow & Company, Inc. • New York

Inquiries should be addressed to
Greenwillow Books, 105 Madison Avenue,
New York, N.Y. 10016.
Printed in the United States of America.

10   9   8   7   6   5   4   3   2   1

Thanks are due to Dwain Parrack
for his meticulous explanation
of birdcatching techniques and
to F. B. Bang for background research
material provided.

Library of Congress
Cataloging in Publication Data

Bang, Betsy.
The old woman and the rice thief.
Summary: Retells a traditional
Bengali tale in which an
old woman outwits a rice thief.
[1.   Folklore, Bengali]
I.   Bang, Molly.   II.   Title.
PZ8.1.B2260p   [398.2]   [E]   76-30671
ISBN 0-688-80098-X
ISBN 0-688-84098-1 lib. bdg.

To Dr. Farida Huq
and her husband, Rafique ul Huq,
for their generosity
and continued support

There was once an old woman who loved rice. Every morning she boiled half of her rice and left it soaking in a pot of cold water. With the other half she made *muri*, and put some of it on the oven to stay warm. In this way she always had cold boiled rice in the soaking pot and warm puffed rice on the oven.

The old woman was content until a thief appeared. He came each night and stole some cold boiled rice from the soaking pot and some muri from the oven.

So the old woman took her walking stick and set out
to complain to the Raja.

Soon she came to the edge of a pond. In the pond
was a scorpion-fish who said to her, "Old woman,
where are you going?"

"Every night a thief steals my rice. I am going to
complain to the Raja."

The scorpion-fish said, "On your way home, take
me with you and you will be glad that you did."

"Ach-chha," said the old woman.

And she walked along the road until she came to a wood-apple tree.
A wood-apple had fallen to the ground and it said, "Old woman,
where are you going?"

"Every night a thief steals my rice, so I am going to tell the Raja."
The wood-apple said, "On your way home, take me with you
and you will be glad that you did."
"Ach-chha," said the old woman.

A little farther along she saw a razor. The razor said,
"Old woman, where are you going?"
"Every night a thief steals my rice, and I am going to
complain to the Raja."
The razor said, "On your way home, take me with you
and you will be glad that you did."
"Ach-chha," said the old woman.

As she walked along, there was a cowpat lying in the road, and when the old woman stepped over it, the cowpat said, "Old woman, where are you going?"

"Every night a thief steals my rice, so I am on my way
to tell the Raja."
"On your way home, take me with you and you will be
glad that you did."
"Ach-chha," said the old woman.

Just before the old woman reached the Raja's palace,
she saw an alligator in the river. The alligator said,
"Old woman, where are you going?"

"Every night a thief eats my rice, and I am going to make a complaint to the Raja."

The alligator said, "On your way home, take me with you and you will be glad that you did."

"Ach-chha," said the old woman.

When she came to the Raja's palace, she found that the Raja was out

hunting tigers and that she would have to come back another day.

On her way home she picked up the alligator, and the cowpat and the

razor, the wood-apple and the scorpion-fish and put them in her sack.

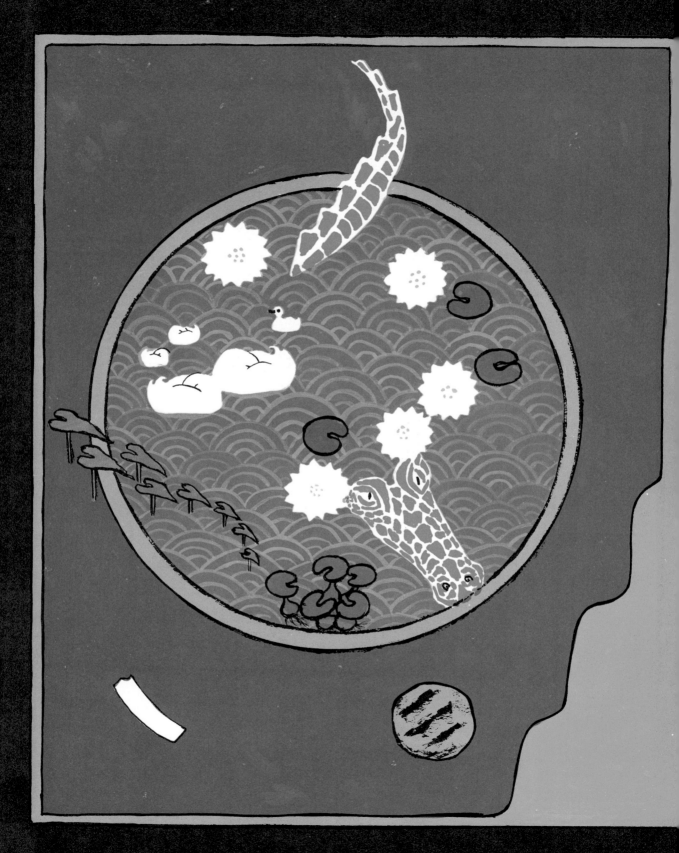

When they came to her house, the alligator said, "Leave
me here in your pond."

The cowpat said, "Put me at the bottom of the stairs."

The razor said, "Put me down in the grass near the cowpat."

The wood-apple said, "Put me in the oven."

The scorpion-fish said, "Put me in the soaking pot with
the cold boiled rice."

Then the old woman had a supper of muri and said
good night to them all and went to bed.

In the middle of the night the thief came.
He sneaked inside and reached into the soaking pot
to steal some of the cold boiled rice. Inside was the
scorpion-fish! It stung the thief so many times that
he jumped up and down with pain.

Then he went to the oven to steal some muri. When he touched the pot, the wood-apple exploded in his face! The hot seeds stung him all over and the noise scared him out of his wits, so he dashed outside.

But in the dark he slipped on the cowpat, and sat down with a thud on top of the razor.
He scrambled up, squealing, and ran to the pond to wash himself off.

As soon as he touched the water,

the alligator bit him.

"Eee, aiee!" he squealed.

The old woman ran after him, yelling, "Thief! Thief!"
All of this noise woke the neighbors, and everyone
joined in the chase to catch the thief, and they
chased him so far he never came back.

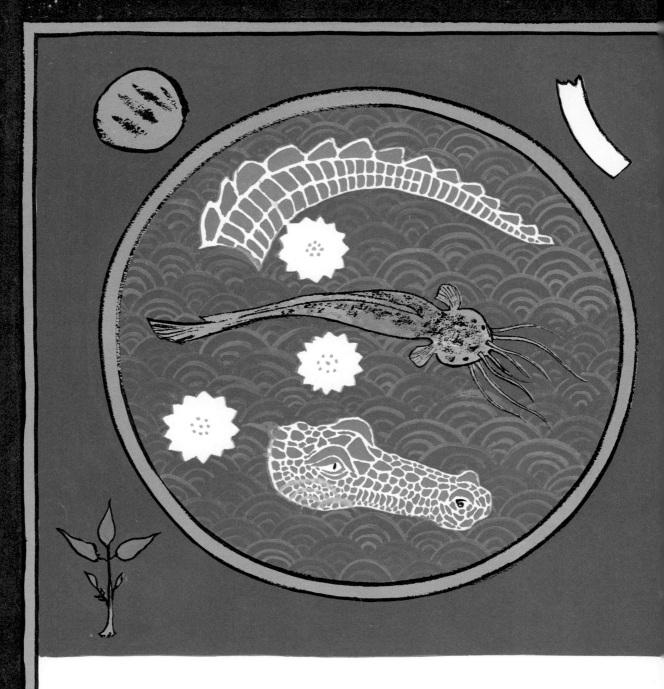

After that, the old woman always had cold boiled rice in the soaking pot and muri on the oven.

কাঁথা